For Kiara, who lights up the world just like the Empire State Building —D.H.

In loving memory of my cousin Lonnie D. Smith, who loved New York City as much as I do (February 14, 1950–January 11, 2005) —J.E.R.

 Published in the United States by Dragonfly Books, an imprint of Random House Children's Books, a division of Random House, Inc., New York. Originally published in hardcover in the United States by Schwartz & Wade Books, an imprint of Random House Children's Books, New York, in 2006.

Dragonfly Books with the colophon is a registered trademark of Random House, Inc.

Visit us on the Web! www.randomhouse.com/kids

Educators and librarians, for a variety of teaching tools, visit us at www.randomhouse.com/teachers

The Library of Congress has cataloged the hardcover edition of this work as follows:
Hopkinson, Deborah.
Sky boys : how they built the Empire State Building / Deborah Hopkinson ;
illustrated by James E. Ransome. — 1st ed.
p. cm.
Summary: In 1931, a boy and his father watch as the world's tallest building,
the Empire State Building, is constructed, step-by-step, near their Manhattan home.
ISBN 978-0-375-83610-7 (hc : alk. paper) — ISBN 978-0-375-93610-4 (lib. bdg.)
[1. Empire State Building (New York, N.Y.)—Design and
construction—Fiction. 2. Skyscrapers—Fiction. 3. Building—Fiction. 4. New York (N.Y.)—History—1898–1951—Fiction.]
I. Ransome, James E., ill. II. Title.
PZ7.H778125Sk 2006
[E]—dc22
2005010852

ISBN 978-0-375-86541-1 (pbk.)

MANUFACTURED IN CHINA

10 9 8 7

First Dragonfly Books Edition

SKY BOYS

How They Built the Empire State Building

Written by Deborah Hopkinson
& illustrated by James E. Ransome

dragonfly books new york

It's the end of winter,
and your pop's lost his job.
So every morning before school
you scour the streets for firewood,
hunched down in an icy wind.

G. ROMEO

But look!
Here's a pile of wood,
free for the taking—
all carted off
from that old hotel
they tore down at
Thirty-fourth and Fifth.

Six hundred men
are working there—
leveling, shoveling, hauling,
clearing the rubble away.
They're getting ready to make
something new,

bold,

SOARING.

A symbol of hope

in the darkest of times.

A building,
clean and simple
and straight as a pencil.
And tall,
so tall it will scrape the sky.

You drag your pop along to see, and
tell him what you've heard on the street.
"Mr. Raskob wants to build
the tallest skyscraper in the world," you say,
"taller even than Mr. Chrysler's building!
They say it'll be done by next May.
Think they can build it that fast, Pop?"
"Things are so bad, it seems
foolish to even try," he replies.
Then he sees your face and adds,
"Course, you never know. . . ."

So let the race begin!

First come rumbling flatbed trucks,
bundles of steel on their backs,
like a gleaming, endless river
surging through
the concrete canyons of Manhattan.

This steel is strong and new,
only eighty hours old,
barely cooled
from the fiery furnaces of Pittsburgh.

Before your eyes a steel forest appears.
Two hundred and ten massive columns,
lifted by derricks
and set onto concrete piers
sunk fifty-five feet down
to hard-rock bottom.

Columns so firm and strong,
they can bear the full weight
of this giant-to-be:
365,000 tons.

Then it's the sky boys' show.
Derrick men
hoisting, swinging,
easing each beam into place.
High overhead they crawl
like spiders on steel,
spinning their giant web in the sky.

Watch out, sky boys—
don't slip in the rain
or let the wind whisk you away!

Wouldn't you love to be one of them,
the breeze in your face
and your muscles as strong
as the girder you ride?

Or you could be a water boy,
climbing high with your bucket
to bring the sky boys a drink.
They'd laugh and call out,
"Keep your eyes on the beam, water boy,
and don't look down!"

As each beam is placed,
the riveting gang is there
to fasten the frame together.
Four men work as one.

First man,
the Heater,
gets the rivet
red-hot in the forge
and tosses it up quick.
(A throw of fifty feet
is nothing to him.)

Second man,
the Catcher,
snares the rivet in his funneled tin can,
fishes it out with tongs,
and sticks it in the hole.

Third man,
the Bucker-up,
keeps the rivet
nice and steady
with his bar.

Fourth man,
the Gunman,
hammers it into the steel,
good and hard.

Toss-catch-steady-pound.
Toss-catch-steady-pound.
One or two rivets a minute,
five hundred rivets a day.

At the same time
other workers use six hoists
to carry eight-thousand-pound loads
of wood and steel
right to where they're needed.
And on each floor
hand-powered railcars on tracks
move limestone, pipes, and wires around.

To make the work easier
there are temporary elevators,
water tanks, and, yes, toilets,
five lunch stands, and even a restaurant.
No need to leave the job.
Get hot beef stew and coffee here,
on the unfinished forty-seventh floor!

In this new, ingenious,
assembly-line construction
each man works as fast as he can,
knowing that down below
a hundred jobless men are ready

to take over his spot in a flash.
Yet knowing, too,
that the quicker he finishes,
the sooner he'll be back in line himself,
waiting and desperate for work.

From your spot on the sidewalk
you watch the building take shape,

bit by bit, piece by piece,
like a giant, real-life puzzle,

JUNE

JULY

rising four and a half
stories each week.

In November the sky boys give a cheer.
The skeleton has a skin—
all one hundred and two stories are done!

AUGUST NOVEMBER

And by March the mast on top makes
this the tallest building in the world.

5:42pm MARCH 18, 1931

Like a general launching an attack,
the builder sends in more men—
bricklayers, masons, carpenters,
electricians, plumbers,
all hammering, nailing,
wiring, and cutting
morning till night,
week after week,
month after month.

May 1, 1931: opening day.
Finished in record time!
Sixty thousand tons of steel,
ten million bricks,
two thousand tons of marble,
sixty-five hundred windows,
seventy miles of water pipes,
eighteen hundred and sixty stairs.
One year and forty-five days,
seven million man-hours,
more than three thousand men—
a triumph of speed, safety, and efficiency,
and something else, too: beauty.

The ribbon is cut, the crowds swarm in.

"Amazing! Spectacular!"

"Now the world can see

what New York City's all about!"

Outside, Pop has a big surprise.
"Let's go on up," he suggests with a grin.
"I been puttin' our pennies aside."

The crowd sweeps you into
the marbled lobby, a tall, grand lady,
clothed head to toe in rich, glowing colors.
On the center wall
a silhouette glitters like a jewel:
the Empire State Building,
pride of New York City!

To go to the top,
it's a buck for adults, two bits for kids.
Hop on board for the longest elevator ride of your life.
Just swallow if your ears start to hurt.

In no time you're there,
but even on tiptoe you can't see a thing.
Then *whoosh!* You're up on Pop's back.
"Gee whiz!" you shout.
"We're on top of the world."
Pop shakes his head, disbelieving.
"If we can do this, we can do anything," he says.

Itching to see it all,
you jump down and race round the deck.
North and south and east and west,
all Manhattan lies at your feet.
"Say, Pop," you call,
"do you think there's a kid just like me
way down there,
looking at us up here?"

After a while the sun slips away;
tiny lights and stars flicker on.
Bright threads of taxis
lace the darkness below;
the great city shimmers and hums.

All around, folks are starting to leave.
You beg, "Please, Pop, a few minutes more?"
But it's time. So, with one last look,
you head down to earth.

On the long walk home
you're fuzzy with sleep,
holding tight to your father's rough hand.

But then at the corner you turn
and stop short in surprise.
"Look, Pop, we can still see it from here!"

Oh, how it lights up the night.

A Note About the Story

The Empire State Building, at 350 Fifth Avenue in New York City, is one of the most famous buildings in the world. When it was completed during the Great Depression, in 1931, it immediately became the world's tallest building, beating out the 77-story, 1,046-foot-tall Chrysler Building, finished in 1930. Although the Empire State Building is no longer the tallest in the world, it remains one of the most beloved landmarks in the United States and is a New York City and National Historic Landmark.

To this day, the construction of the Empire State Building ranks among the most amazing accomplishments in American architecture. The skyscraper was the brainchild of a successful businessman named John J. Raskob, who, along with Al Smith, former governor of New York, was determined to beat the competition and build the tallest building in the world. (James Ransome depicts Al Smith in this book, proudly greeting visitors in front of the Empire State Building on opening day along with his wife and two grandchildren.) The architect, William F. Lamb, of Shreve, Lamb & Harmon, based his design on the clean, simple lines of a pencil. Using innovative building techniques, the contracting firm Starrett Brothers and Eken set records for the incredible efficiency and speed of the construction.

The Empire State Building itself is 1,250 feet high, with a total height of 1,454 feet if you add the 204-foot-tall television antenna erected in 1950. Millions of people each year visit the building, which has been featured in dozens of movies and is also a favorite place to get engaged and even to get married. To learn more about the Empire State Building, visit its official Web site at www.esbnyc.com.

The Empire State Building is my favorite building. I love standing on the observation deck on the eighty-sixth floor. Just as exciting is to turn while crossing a busy Manhattan street and catch a sudden glimpse of the building, majestic and serene. It's like meeting a trusted old friend.

Acknowledgments and Sources

The statistics in this story are those listed on the official Empire State Building Web site. Perhaps the most comprehensive book for adults about the Empire State Building is John Tauranac's *The Empire State Building: The Making of a Landmark* (New York: Scribner, 1995). *Building the Empire State*, edited by Carol Willis and Donald Friedman (New York: W. W. Norton, 1998), contains the contractors' rediscovered record of the building's construction. For the image of the sky boys as spiders, I am indebted to an article in the *New Yorker* (quoted in Tauranac, p. 208). The term "sky boy" appears in the title of one of Lewis Hine's photographs of the construction, which are available as post-cards in *Lewis Hine: The Empire State Building Photographs* (Rohnert Park, Calif.: Pomegranate Artbooks, 1992). The term was also used by Earl Sparling in an article in the *World-Telegram* (quoted in Tauranac, p. 225).

The photographs that appear on the endpapers were taken between 1930 and 1931 by Lewis Wickes Hine and appear courtesy of the Empire State Building Archive, Avery Architectural and Fine Arts Library, Columbia University.

Special thanks to Lydia Ruth, director of public relations for the Empire State Building, for taking the time to read the manuscript, and also to Carol Willis, founder, director, and curator of the Skyscraper Museum, www. skyscraper.org.